BRILLIANT
THE DINOSAUR

BRILLIANT
THE DINOSAUR

RICHARD STILGOE
ILLUSTRATED BY DAVID MELLING

PAVILION

First published in Great Britain in 1994 by
PAVILION BOOKS LIMITED
26 Upper Ground, London SE1 9PD

Typeset in Palatino

Designed by Nigel Partridge

A CIP catalogue record for this book is available from the British Library.

ISBN 1 85793 283 8

Printed in Italy by Imago

2 4 6 8 10 9 7 5 3 1

This book can be ordered direct from the publisher. Please contact the
Marketing Department. But try your bookshop first.

CONTENTS

INTRODUCTION

THE WHERE, WHEN AND WHO OF IT, BUT NOT YET THE WHY.

Clademouth is a small town on the South Coast of Devon. It's not a fishing village, and it's not a holiday resort, it just happens to have been plonked down by the sea, at the mouth of the river Clade.

The river Clade is quite pretty when it's a young, bright, leaping stream on Dartmoor. But gradually it grows bigger and gets a job supplying water to a town. Then it gets older and wider and slower, but just manages to reach Clademouth and retire into the sea.

Many of the residents of Clademouth are retired. Nobody knows why, just at the moment when people get too old to want to swim or build sandcastles, they decide to go and live by the seaside. But they do.

Because Clademouth is a non-fishing, non-holiday resort full of retired people, it is a very boring place for children. (It is also a very boring place for grown-ups, but the grown-ups call that 'peace and quiet'.) These are some of the people who find Clademouth boring:

MR AND MRS BANKS (MUM & DAD)

Mr Banks is a printer, and prints the Clademouth *Clarion*, which is a free newspaper paid for by advertisements for electric cars and bicycles in good condition (though not *quite* such good condition as the advertisements say they are in).

Mrs Banks is a music teacher. She teaches the piano to children whose parents always wanted to learn, but haven't the time now so make their children learn instead. Sometimes she teaches at home, sometimes at Clademouth School.

MRS BRAY (HARRIET)

Harriet Bray is an English teacher. She was married once, but isn't now. She is Mum's best friend.

MR BRIDGES

Mr Bridges teaches Science at the school. He is not married to anyone. He would like to be married to Mum. This is a pity, what with Harriet fancying him quite a lot and being available, and Mum not fancying him at all and being married to Dad. (Quite happily, too, or as happily as anyone married to the printer of the Clademouth *Clarion* expects to be.) Mum is mainly happy because of:

JESSICA (15), FERGUS (14) AND TIM (10) BANKS

These are Mum's children. Jessica is tall and clever, Fergus is small but strong and funny and Tim is rather worried by things. They have two next door neighbours who are also great friends, and their names are DIXIE (15, pretty and naughty) and BILLY (14, freckled and naughtier).

There are also large numbers of other children and grown-ups in Clademouth, but giving all their names would only cause confusion.

One thing they have in common is that they all listen to Radio Sun, the local radio station, on which the presenters try and pretend that life in Clademouth isn't boring at all. No one believes them, but it's nice of them to try.

At the time we're talking about, which is just a few years from now, South Devon is enjoying its third long, hot summer in a row. (Radio Sun is relieved, because its name sounds silly when the weather's bad.) But all that is about to change, because, at the very moment we start paying attention to the doings of Clademouth, the least boring thing ever to happen there is about to happen.

ONE

A DREADFUL WEATHER FORECAST – FEARS ABOUT THE SEA WALL
– SOME DREADFUL WEATHER.

'Radio Sun, Radio Sun!' sings the radio, and Mum, sweltering in the hot afternoon, wishes irons didn't have to be so hot for cotton. But she goes on ironing Tim's white shirt which he has *got* to have for the school concert.

'And it's over to Janice at our weather desk,' says the radio.

'It certainly is, Simon,' says Janice brightly, 'and a bit of a surprise for all of you jolly jack tars (Simon, in the studio, looks despairingly up to heaven, but of course Mum can't see this) sailing about on the briny in all this luvverly sunshine. It's gonna get mighty breezy out there tonight. We have gale warnings in Portland, Plymouth, Fastnet, Finisterre, Biscay – ooh, all sorts of places. I'm sure you old salts know where I mean. And not just gales. It says storm force ten, possibly violent storm force eleven later. So, splice those mainbraces, chaps and chapesses, because it's going to be windier than a dog full of beans. Simon.'

'Terrific, Janice. So, plenty of fresh air tonight, but the fine weather holding on. Afternoon temperatures 28°, that's 82° in the old money, and here's one from a few years back when even your Uncle Simon was young.'

Mum sang along. The words of songs learnt when you're young stay with you forever. In the studio, Simon poured Janice a cup of decaf, and in the Atlantic just off Finisterre the worst storm for seven years danced furiously towards them.

There was only a light breeze on the cliff as Jessica, Fergus, Dixie and Billy walked home from school. They weren't supposed to be there.

'You're not supposed to be here,' said Tim, running to catch up with them. He was still at the middle school, which got out a bit later, so he always had to run to catch up with them. Once he *had* caught up with them he still had to run, because his legs weren't as long as theirs so he had to move them more often to compensate. 'We're all not supposed to be here because the cliff might fall down any minute.'

'If it was going to fall down it would have fallen down ages ago,' said Billy.

'For someone in the future, ages ago might be now,' said Fergus. The others tried to work that out. 'Come away from the edge,' said Tim. 'It's dangerous.'

So they all stood along the edge of the cliff and hit it with their heels, sending clods of red clay tumbling on to the shingle in a very satisfying way. Despite the breeze, it was very hot indeed.

Mr Banks sat in the bar of the Duck of Windsor. Well, yes, the Duke of Windsor really, but the 'e' had fallen off the sign years ago. Even though the new owner had replaced it, the locals were too pleased with the name to change it, so the Duck of Windsor is what it was always called.

'You're not supposed to be here,' said Mr Banks, as Mr Bridges walked in. Mr Bridges jumped – had Mr Banks discovered his guilty passion for Mum? 'Isn't it Science Club on Tuesday evenings?'

Mr Bridges looked relieved. 'Oh. Yes. Normally. Not tonight. Lab. technician's away. On a course. Government thing. Sent them home. Early.'

'Just as well, if we're getting hit by this storm,' said Mr Banks, sipping his drink and wondering why low alcohol lager tasted like fizzy aluminium.

'What storm?' Mr Bridges hadn't been listening to the radio, because he'd been doing Introduction to Chemistry

with the first years, which needed all your concentration if loss of life was to be avoided.

'Radio Sun. They had something about it. And the BBC man too. Force ten, occasionally eleven. Tonight, if it hits us. May go up the Irish Sea or it may fizzle out. Remember the last one?'

Mr Bridges nodded. 'Three years ago. Very lucky. Low tide. Waves didn't hit the cliff. I've told them.'

'Told them what?' asked Mr Banks. 'And who?'

'The council. The sea wall. They won't do it.'

'Oh, that.' Mr Banks remembered Mr Bridges' hobby-horse. The Clademouth cliffs were soft clay, and since the shingle bank a hundred metres offshore had been dredged to get gravel for the M237, Mr Bridges had maintained (to anyone who'd listen) that a spring tide and a bad storm would eat away the bottom of the cliff. He believed the only way to save the cliff was to build a sea wall of re-inforced concrete (a sketch of which he would produce from his pocket at the slightest provocation). The man at the council offices knew his handwriting by now, and threw away the envelopes without opening them.

'Have another?' asked Mr Banks, changing the subject.

'My shout,' said Mr Bridges. 'Is that a Rhinegold?' Mr Banks agreed that his glass of fizzy metal was called Rhinegold.

'Same again?' asked Mr Bridges.

Mr Banks said no, a Scotch please, and Mr Bridges looked relieved because that was what he wanted too. Anyone who has counted all the first years in to Introduction to Chemistry and counted them all back at the end deserves a little prize.

At Radio Sun, Janice shared Simon's paper cup of Italian white wine and wondered if Simon would look better without his moustache. Simon had already decided Janice would look better without hers.

At home, Mum had a glass of something with Greek writing on the label which she'd won on the bottle stall at the fête in aid of the school laser.

By eleven o'clock, everyone was where they were supposed to be. Tim was asleep, with a little frown on his face. Fergus was asleep. Billy and Dixie were asleep next door. Jessica was putting Zitsoff on the bigger of her spots, and reading *The Elephant Man*, which cheered her up about her skin. Simon and Janice, in front of the electric logs in Janice's maisonette had decided each other's moustaches were not really worth worrying about, and Mum and Dad were trying to find their places in the books they'd been reading for the last two months.

'No sign of this storm.' That was Mum.

'Neil Bridges says it'll bring the cliff down. No sea wall.'

'I've told them. Council. Will they listen?' Mum's impression of Mr Bridges was rather good – she had heard his sea defence theories as often as Dad.

'House would be more valuable,' said Dad. 'If the cliff fell down, we'd be on the sea front.'

Mum laughed at this, in an encouraging sort of way, and patted Dad playfully on the knee.

At three-thirty in the morning the earth moved.

The wind blew at eighty miles an hour, the tide rose to its highest height, and the livid waters of the sea bit great chunks from the Clademouth cliffs, so that they fell into the channel, making a great red boiling minestrone of earth and shingle which abraded yet more of the cliff, until a vast, thirty-metre-wide slice of cliff slid seaward. It stopped, as it met old strata of sandstone that storms could not move. But it left behind it a gap – a chasm behind the new shape of the cliff, full of earth, bits of the road by the Banks's house, half a pedestrian crossing, Dad's electric car and a smell that had not been smelt on the earth for 65 million years.

TWO

AFTER THE HURRICANE – A CAVERN FULL OF STRANGE NOISES
– MATERNAL CONCERN.

'We're not supposed to be here,' said Tim.
'Don't be silly,' said Jessica. 'This place hasn't been here before, so we can't have been forbidden to be in it.' And she switched on her torch, and led Fergus and Tim into the new, dark ravine.

'Pooh!' said Tim, and held his nose.

Janice was sitting under a polythene sheet in the Radio Sun studios. Simon, a small plaster on his forehead, was hanging over his microphone, knowing that for once he was in the right place at the right time.

'Eight twenty-three,' said Simon, 'and I know a lot of you have heard this before, but there are people tuning in all the time – most of you, I guess, on battery radios until the guys at Powergen get their wires uncrossed. So, what's been going on? Early this morning, a storm – a violent storm, force eleven on the Beaufort Scale . . .'

'That's right, Simon,' interrupted Janice (who could see her place in history being snowploughed aside by Simon). 'Gusting up to very high speeds indeed.'

'. . . thank you, Janice. Our weatherperson, Janice Reeves, who I personally know stayed awake throughout the night to experience the primeval forces unleashed by nature. Now, if you'll excuse us, listener, I have National Network Radio on the other line because today Clademouth is the centre of where it's at – or, if you live on the cliff, where it *was*. So while we link up with them, here's a stormy bit of Vivaldi from the violin of Sir Nigel Kennedy.'

In the kitchen Mum listened to the musical downpour

coming out of the portable, and wondered how she was supposed to cope without electricity. When the storm struck in the night she had been terrified. The sudden change from quiet sleep to raging noise all round. The unknownness of it. She had got up and gone to count the children, and found a man in Tim's bedroom. It was Dad, who had woken before her and gone on the same mission. He put a pyjamaed arm round her, and it was comforting to find that he was shivering too.

Tim stayed asleep, as did Fergus in the upper bunk and Jessica next door. Mum and Dad had gone back to bed and listened to the world outside magimixing itself. And now this morning the Magimix didn't work, nor did the microwave, and Mum wasn't even sure where the spare batteries were for the radio.

'Cooee!' said a voice, and Harriet came in with a thermos. Mum was pleased to see both of them.

'Why aren't you at school?' she said.

'Difficult to know where to go,' said Harriet, pouring tea. 'The school's scattered all over the town. The craft and design portacabin's upside down in the cemetery and the staff hut was last seen floating out to sea, still with all of 4B's essays about Columbus in it. Haven't you been out to have a look?'

Mum hadn't. Dad had – he'd gone to work quite early, because for once there might be something to put in the Clademouth *Clarion* that wasn't a picture of a budgerigar sitting on a cat's head or the results of the flower show. The children had gone out early too, before the radio had told Mum enough to make her stop them. Mum drank her tea, and started to shake. Harriet put a hand on her arm. 'I told them to be careful,' said Mum, 'but they never listen.' 'Yes they do,' said Harriet, who could recognize the need for a comforting fib every now and then.

Fergus had brought with him the big metal torch that

must *never* be moved from the shelf inside the kitchen door, and a pocket compass which (though he hadn't yet realized this) always pointed at the big metal torch. Jessica had brought her radio, which had mentioned Clademouth three times on the national news. Fergus came over to it to listen, and the compass couldn't decide which was more attractive, the torch or the radio, so went round and round in circles.

'At Clademouth in Devon . . .'

'That's four mentions,' said Tim.

'. . . sections of the cliff have collapsed, and electricity and telephone lines are down. Several school buildings have been destroyed, but there is no news of any casualties. Number Ten Downing Street has sent a message of sympathy, and Mr Coe says he hopes to visit the town very soon. As England's batsmen follow on against the Falklands . . .'

A sudden noise caught their attention – the quick patter of falling earth and gravel as something moved above and behind them.

'Who's that?' said Fergus.

'Princess Beatrice, . . .' said the radio, before Jessica turned it off. More bits of rubble rolled past them, and Dixie and Billy arrived.

'What's all this then?' said Dixie.

'I think it was Tim,' said Billy. 'I think Tim was kicking the edge of the cliff with his heel and doesn't know his own strength.' 'It *wasn't* me,' said Tim, though he knew Billy was joking. Tim hoped that he'd be like Billy when he was fourteen. Except Billy would be eighteen then. Still, that was the future's problem. Today's problem was the exploration of the ravine.

'Have you explored yet?' asked Billy.

'Not yet,' said Jessica. 'We've only just got here.'

'We'd better be quick,' said Dixie. 'The grown-ups are bound to come nosing around soon.'

'Right then' – this was Fergus – 'Let's go.' Tim shot off into the gloom before the others could tell him to stop. He was light, and sure-footed, and not carrying anything if you didn't count the conker and the fluffy toffee in his left hand trouser pocket. Fergus, Jessica, Dixie and Billy ran after him.

'This way,' said Tim.

'Hang on,' said Fergus. 'You'll need a torch.'

'It's all right,' said Tim, 'I can see a bit. There's a sort of an edge – Ow!' More noise of sliding earth and stones, and Tim's yell mixed in with it as he disappeared. The others rushed forward and fell down the hole as well.

'Where's Tim?' said Billy, urgently.

'Unnummerneef,' said Tim, from underneath him.

They had all slid about six metres, down a steep slope into a deeper part of the new gorge. There was still a little daylight from the opening above them, and yet more further on where the cliff had fallen more untidily. Suddenly, for the first time, the children felt unsafe.

'Look,' said Jessica, 'I think we ought to go back. We'll get into awful trouble if anything happens to Tim.'

'That's just an excuse,' said Tim. 'You're just frightened like the rest of us.'

'All right, I am frightened,' said Jessica. 'All this earth slid about during the night, and who's to say it won't go on sliding about and trap us underneath it. This whole lot could shift at any minute.'

And shift it did. As Jessica spoke, the ground they sat on rippled and flexed, and the slope they had slid down reared up and twisted. The slope was a neck. Fergus ran the light of the torch up it, and found a small pointed head. As the terrified children watched, two yellow eyes opened and blinked. Fergus dropped the torch which must never be moved from the shelf inside the kitchen door, and the children ran towards the light, stumbling over each other and gasping for breath, their lungs tight

with fear. They tumbled out on to the ruins of the cliff, and lay panting in the morning sun. None of them spoke.

But something did. From deep in the cavern, with a strange sound like the wind over milk bottles (which the children had never heard, for milk bottles had not been used for years) they heard something singing. It sang one word, over and over again.

'Frightened. Frightened. Frightened.'

'I'm going to see what it is,' said Jessica. 'The rest of you stay here.'

'Rubbish! We're all going with you,' said Billy.

'Besides,' said Tim, 'we've got to get the torch back.'

THREE

THE DINOSAUR – WORDS AND FEELINGS – THE NAMING OF THE
DINOSAUR – A WHITE LIE.

The dinosaur was frightened. She had only just learned the cry 'frightened' that the small creature had made, but she had known the feeling since she was born. It was the feeling meeting something that might do you harm. She had felt it, and she could tell the small creature had felt it. She guessed the cry went with the feeling, so she cried 'frightened', over and over again, because there had been a storm, and she had woken up after 125 million years in a dark cave full of small creatures who squeaked and had hair.

Slowly and painfully (for she had not moved for eons) she straightened her four fat legs, and stretched her long, strong neck. Stones and clay rumbled down the sides of the cavern and bounced against her leathery flanks. Carefully, she turned round to face the light. The fissure through which the squeaky creatures had fled was too far away even for her long neck to investigate. But she could hear their voices and their steps, and see the shadows changing as they moved through the passage. They were coming back. They were still frightened, but she could sense another feeling as well – another feeling she knew.

'Come on,' said Jessica, 'be brave.'

'I don't *feel* very brave,' said Dixie.

The dinosaur knew 'brave'. She had had to be brave before. Again, the cry was new to her. Perhaps all of the small creatures' feelings had cries. She tried it.

'Brave!' she said. 'Brave!' And then, as she felt the creatures' reaction, 'Frightened! Frightened!'

'It's an echo,' said Tim.

Fergus shook his head. 'No, it's not – it's copying us.'

'It's very confusing,' said Tim.

'Ssh!' said Fergus. 'I'm thinking.'

So many different waves were reaching the dinosaur now she was unsure which cry fitted. She made a guess.

'Confusing!' she said, 'Confusing!'

'I've got it,' said Jessica. 'It's our feelings – it senses our feelings.'

'What does?' said Tim.

'Whatever it is in there. It knows what we're feeling.'

'How does it know the words?' asked Billy.

'We say them. When we're frightened we *say* we are.'

'I'm going to try it,' said Billy, and took a pace forward into the cavern. Shoving his shoulders back, he boomed, 'Confident! Confident!'

There was a pause.

'Frightened,' said the dinosaur.

'There you are,' said Jessica, 'it knows what you're really feeling.'

'Yes, but what is it?' asked Dixie.

'Oh, come on,' said Fergus. 'Let's go and look.' And he marched forward, the other children struggling behind him.

It took some time for their eyes to re-adjust to the gloom. It took a little more time to realize what it was they were looking at, for the dinosaur nearly filled the cavern, and they could not see right to the far end of her. But the two browny-grey tree trunk legs and the long neck with its pointed, duck-like head (and still those yellow eyes blinking worriedly at them) left them with only one possible conclusion.

'It's a dinosaur,' said Dixie.

The dinosaur could not say, 'It's five children,' because she had never seen a child and could only count 'none, one, some, lots.' Nor did she know the words surprise and astonishment, which were the emotions reaching her from

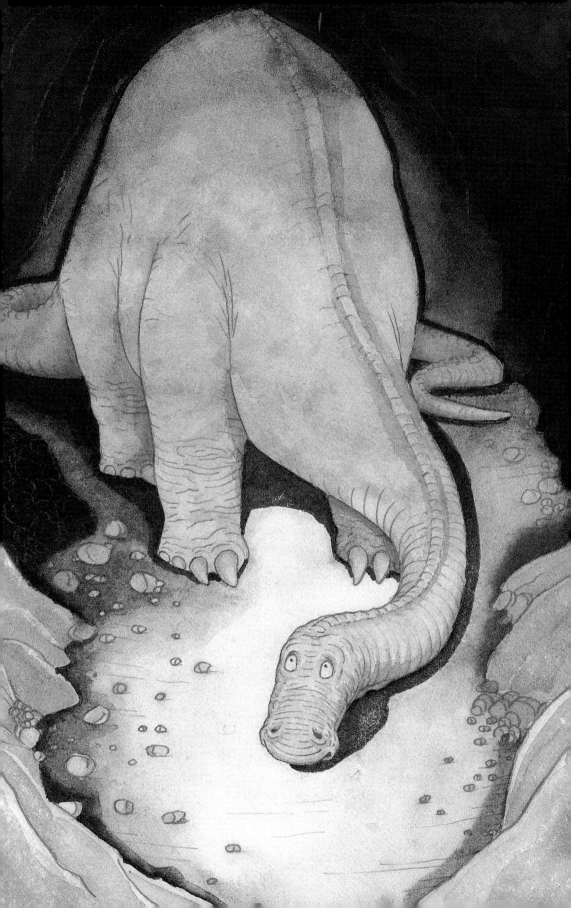

the children. She guessed that, as before, the cry they made went with the emotion, but she did not say 'dinosaur' because she was no longer surprised. She was cold, worried and hungry and beginning to wonder if the position she was in was the fault of the squeaky creatures. Were they trying to hurt her, and should she hurt them first?

Tim then did a helpful thing. Concentrating very hard, he walked forward until he was right underneath the dinosaur's head. He looked up at it.

'Peaceful,' he said, 'peaceful.'

With a great and grateful sigh, the dinosaur repeated the word and lowered her head to his level. A forked tongue slid from her lips and stroked his bare knee. To her surprise he was warm to the touch. Tim put out a hand and stroked the horny skin on her head. 'Peaceful,' they both said. The other children gathered round.

'It's a Tyrannosaurus Rex,' said Billy.

'It's a Brontosaurus,' said Fergus.

'That's right,' said Dixie. 'It's a Brontosaurus.'

'There's no such thing,' said Tim, still stroking. 'The Brontosaurus was a fake. The scientists put the wrong skull on the skeleton. It never existed. It could be an Apatosaurus or an Iguanadon, but I think it's a Diplodocus.'

'How do you know all that?' asked Dixie.

'He did a project on dinosaurs,' said Jessica. 'It got two merits and a gold star.' (Big sisters can sometimes forget to put their little brothers down, and be quite proud of them.)

'Does it *know* it's a Diplodocus?' asked Billy.

'Of course not,' said Jessica. 'There wasn't Latin or Greek or English or anything then.'

'We should tell it what it is, and who we are,' suggested Fergus. 'Like hostages do. If it knows our names, it's less likely to hurt us.'

'I'm sure it won't hurt us,' said Tim, stroking the head.

'Peaceful,' said the dinosaur.

One by one the children pointed to themselves and said their names. After all five had done this, they pointed at the dinosaur, and said 'Diplodocus'. They repeated the process several times.

The dinosaur was confused. She could recognize frightened, and peaceful and brave. The children were giving off all of these. She could recognize confusing. But these cries were all different, and didn't match the feelings. What did their pointing claws mean? It was very difficult.

'Hold on,' said Jessica, 'if I'm right about it recognizing feelings, then we'll be confusing it . . .'

'So it'll think Dixie means scared,' said Dixie.

'Frightened,' said the dinosaur, remembering a word and dropping it hopefully into the conversation.

'Exactly,' said Jessica. 'Let me try this.' And she picked up a stone, because stones have no feelings. Not even stones that have bounced off a born-again dinosaur. She pointed at the stone, and then at the dinosaur.

'Stone,' she said. 'Diplodocus. Stone. Diplodocus.'

And a light went on in the dinosaur's tiny brain. She raised her head and looked straight at the stone.

'Stone,' she said. Then she tried to point at herself, by raising a foot.

'Look,' said Jessica, 'it's *brilliant.*'

'Brilliant,' said the dinosaur, and fell over.

Though the children did not realize it, they were the first people ever to see a dinosaur fall over. She missed them, so it was quite funny. They pointed at her, and laughed.

This was the best cry the dinosaur had heard so far, and the happiness that went with it was by far the best feeling. She lay on her side, quite relaxed, but still unsure about whether she was called 'hahaha' or 'Brilliant' or that other word she hadn't quite caught.

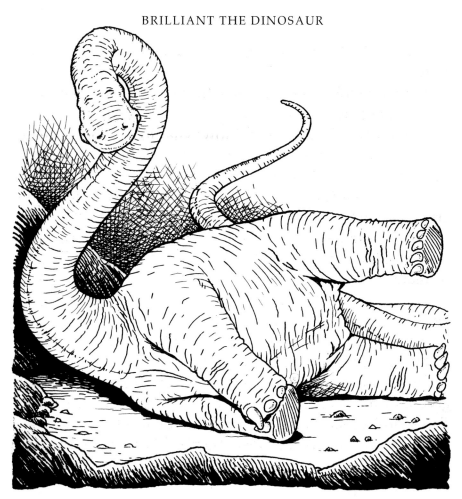

The squeaky creatures started jabbering excitedly.

'How did it get here?'

'How long has it been here?'

'Is it real?'

'Is it a young one or an old one?'

'Should we tell Mum?'

'Or Dad?'

They fell silent. They all knew, without any more need for speech than the dinosaur had, that the finding of a dinosaur was one of those things where grown-ups could not quite be trusted to behave in the right way.

'We must go home,' said Fergus. 'This is the first place they'll look for us. If they come here, they'll find the Diplodocus.'

'They'll look in here anyway, because it's new,' said Billy.

'No they won't,' said Fergus, 'because we will tell them we found something in here.'

'We mustn't. They won't know what to say to it. They'll annoy it. It's too big to let it get annoyed.' Tim sometimes managed to put things very well.

'We will tell them,' continued Fergus, 'that in this cavern we have found an unexploded bomb . . .'

'. . . and they won't come in, but will put barricades and notices outside to stop people,' said Dixie. 'That's brilliant.'

'And sort of true really,' said Tim, who liked things to be true if at all possible.

'What about when the army arrive to defuse it and find a Diplodocus which talks?' asked Dixie.

Fergus looked cross. 'I know it's not perfect. But it'll give us time. We must have time to think, and to study Tim's project so we know more about it. Now come on. We've found an unexploded bomb. It's grey, and it has fins.'

'Is it ticking?'

'Definitely ticking. Let's go and tell Mum about it.'

He led them out of the cave. Before they left, Tim turned to the dinosaur.

'I'm glad we found you,' he said.

'Brilliant,' said the dinosaur.

FOUR

GROWN-UPS' LACK OF IMAGINATION – A CONVINCING BOMB
IMPRESSION – THE LOST PROJECT.

'What size was this bomb?' asked Dad.

'Big,' said Fergus.

'Huge,' said Jessica.

'And ticking,' said Tim.

'A barricade,' said Dad. 'That's what we need. And a notice.'

Mum looked worried. 'Perhaps we ought to let Neil Bridges have a look at it. The children might be wrong.'

The children looked even more worried. If Mr Bridges went into the cave all was lost. He might not be about to win a Nobel Prize, but Mr Bridges was bright enough to tell a Diplodocus from an unexploded bomb.

He couldn't. It's not that grown-ups are particularly stupid, it's just that they have had their imaginations dulled by time. If you are forty years old, you have walked on eight times as many cracks in the pavement as somebody who is five years old. But you still have not met a bear. These years of boring experience get you into a frame of mind where you no longer expect to meet a bear. It's not just eight times less likely, it's worse. When you tread on your first crack, you expect to meet a bear. You don't meet one. The second crack, still no bear. By the third crack, you think it's half as likely. If every two bear-less cracks halve your expectation, then after forty cracks your expectations are divided by 1,048,576. This is what happens to grown-ups. Years and years of not meeting bears mean that when they do meet one they don't recognize it. They expect the boring option. And because they expect the boring option they are not prepared for the odd

28

surprise. Which is why things like stink bombs make children laugh and make grown-ups slightly unhappy.

An unexploded bomb isn't a very boring option, but it
was what Mr Bridges had been told to expect. And it did
look very convincing. A grey, dirty, bullet-shaped nose
sticking out of the ground. And it was ticking. This surprised the children, but pleased them. It also surprised Mr
Bridges, and relieved him, because it meant he didn't
have to go any nearer, but could deliver his judgment
from a safe distance.

'Bomb,' he said. 'Definitely. Bomb. Second World War.
Land- slide must have tripped it. Set it going. Better
move. Could go up any time.' And they all trooped out of
the dark cave, and a barrier was erected with 'Danger.
Unexploded Bomb' on it, which made it true as far as
most people were concerned.

'Why was it ticking?' said Tim. 'Did one of you go back
and teach it to tick?'

'I went back,' said Dixie, 'with an alarm clock. I buried
it in there. Then I drew a picture of a bomb's nose and
showed it to the dinosaur, and it sort of made itself a hole
and stuck its nose out.'

'Did it say anything?' asked Fergus.

'Only "brilliant",' said Dixie. 'I think it thinks that's its name.'

The others were full of praise for Dixie's initiative, and
impressed by the dinosaur's ability to join in the plot.

'I thought they had very small brains,' said Jessica.

'But very strong instincts,' said Fergus.

'Self-preservation. Trust. It knew Dixie wanted to help.'

'If we're going to help it survive,' said Jessica, 'we need
to know more about it.'

'Hang on,' said Tim. 'I'll go and get my project. I expect
I can find it.' And he went to ask Mum where it was.

'It was two years ago that he did that project,' Mum said
to Harriet.

'They grow up so quickly,' said Harriet. It was the morning after the discovery of the unexploded bomb, and they were sitting in Mum's kitchen.

'And without all the things *we* grew up with,' she said. 'Remember sea-bathing?'

'Just,' said Harriet. 'When I was very small. But there was only one place left where it was allowed and it was terribly crowded. Then the next year the algae got that beach as well, and it was closed off. We went there in a proper car. With petrol. My Dad used to go to work in it. Every day.'

Mum nodded. 'Mine too. The kids don't know about that. Their father at home with his computer, only going into the office for parties when someone leaves. First time he's met them usually.'

'We were allowed baths in the daytime, weren't we?' said Harriet. 'The school kids have only ever had baths after midnight when the cheap water rate comes on.'

'Twenty-eight television channels.'

'Nothing on any of them.'

'Recycling. We never had recycling.'

'We did. I used to take the bottles to the bottle bank.'

'I mean, we didn't have recycling like now. Human stuff on the garden. I know the Sewage Digester's supposed to take the smell away, but you can still tell. Jessica wouldn't eat her beans the other day because she said they smelt of Fergus.'

'They grow up so quickly.'

'They do.'

'I blame the Government.'

Tim's dinosaur project was found, after a long hunt, propping up a corner of Dad's work station in the office. On the computer screen was an article for the Clademouth *Clarion*. 'After the Hurricane, by Robin Q. Banks.' (The children knew Dad's name was Robin, but didn't mention it because it embarrassed him. Dad's parents hadn't spot-

ted the danger when they named him. It wasn't until Dad, aged five, went to school for the first time that the mistake was spotted. The headmaster said, 'Who are you?' and Dad said, 'I'm Robin Banks,' and the headmaster said, 'Then why aren't you wearing a stocking over your head?' and Dad's life was ruined from that moment until the time he added the initial 'Q' in the middle. Now, instead of making jokes about robbing banks people ask, 'What does the "Q" stand for?' and Dad says, 'They're waiting for the banks to open,' which is as bad a joke as theirs but at least he's making it.)

Tim tugged the folders of papers from under the leg of the desk, and it came down with a bonk. The article on the screen suddenly ran upwards and disappeared, and the word 'erased' replaced them. Tim hoped this didn't matter (especially because he knew that it *did*) and took the project up to Jessica's room, where the others were waiting, surrounded by magazine advertisements for cures for spots, pictures of spotty singers and the poster every teenager in the world had at that time, of the last tree in the Amazon rain forest being ceremoniously felled by a beaming Brazilian president.

'WHEN DINOSAURS ROMED THE EARTH,' it said on the cover of the folder. 'That's wrong,' Billy said. 'I was very young,' said Tim, haughtily.

Fergus, Jessica, Dixie, Billy and Tim studied the dinosaur project. Much of what was in it they knew already – the names and faces of Tyrannosaurus Rex, Triceratops, Stegosaurus and the non-existent Brontosaurus. There were little dinosaurs, no bigger than chickens. Plesiosaurs that might or might not live in Loch Ness, Archaeopteryx who could fly and their own Diplodocus. Tim had drawn a picture of it lumbering about eating trees and apparently being overtaken by an Intercity train ('For comparison of bigness' it said underneath).

The thing that impressed them most was the last paragraph, which Tim had copied out of a book and changed so people wouldn't guess.

'Men and women have lived on this planet for about 100,000 years,' it said. 'We think we're pretty important and successful, and use the word 'dinosaur' to describe a clumsy failure. Well, dinosaurs romed the earth for 160,000,000 (*million*) years. I bet we don't last that long not with pollution.'

'I think it's really excellent,' said Fergus.

'Gosh,' said Tim.

'It *might* be spelt "R-O-M-E-D",' said Billy, 'I'm not sure.'

Tim tried not to look too pleased. Inside he felt like a fiercely shaken fizzy drink can crossed with a light bulb.

FIVE

THE DINOSAUR LEARNS SOME SHAKESPEARE AND THE LOCATION
OF LOCH NESS – THE DIFFERENCE BETWEEN EXTINCT AND
INSTINCT.

Jessica carefully picked her way over the rubble. It was scarcely thirty hours since the hurricane, and already she found it hard to remember what things had looked like before. She could imagine the fallen trees standing again, the pylons re-erected, the sailing boats returned to the sea. (Many were now in people's gardens. One sat in splendour in somebody's swimming pool, where it just fitted across the diagonal. It was to be three months before they got it out, during which time the owner of the pool secretly enjoyed sitting on its deck wearing a yachting cap and reading *Moby Dick*. He really missed it when they finally took it away.) But she couldn't remember the shape the cliff had been. It looked as if the jumble of scree, earth and rock had always been there (which it had, but in a different order). Jessica climbed gingerly down it towards the dinosaur's cavern. It was funny to think that all through her life, there had been a dinosaur asleep under the cliff. She had been pushed on that cliff, toddled, walked and run on it, her footsteps growing heavier and more sure over the years. Never had she thought, 'I wonder if I'm walking on a dinosaur?' Now she knew she had been, she couldn't think of anything else.

The barrier with 'Danger. Unexploded Bomb' on it was unguarded. It was early morning, and everyone was involved in clearing up Clademouth. Jessica walked past it, and through the fissure in the cliff into cold, dim light beyond.

Sand and earth swallow up sound, and the silence in the cavern was deafening. Especially because nothing was

34

ticking. As her eyes widened to bring more twilight in, Jessica saw the bomb sticking out of the sand.

'Clever thing,' she thought. 'It knows it has to keep still.'

Part of the alarm clock was also sticking out of the sand. Mr Bridges hadn't seen it – because he wasn't expecting to see an alarm clock. Jessica picked it up, and walked towards the unexploded bomb. She stroked its nose.

'Hello,' she said.

'Brilliant!' said the unexploded bomb, and opened its eye.

The wave that hit Jessica knocked her two metres backwards. It was as if a huge punch of relief and happiness came from the dinosaur's eye and flattened her as if she were a blade of grass. She got to her feet, and laughed.

'Relief,' she said.

'Relief!' said the dinosaur, from the bottom of its heart (so it took a split-second longer, having to travel some nineteen metres).

The dinosaur looked at Jessica. She liked this one best of the creatures. It hadn't been as confused as the others, and she could sense a strength and a truth in it that was very comforting. The little one was very sweet, of course, but you had to look after it. This one would look after *you*.

Jessica looked at the dinosaur, and pondered the knock-out blow of emotion that had passed her on its way out to sea. They knew the dinosaur had felt their feelings yesterday, but it had been one-way traffic until now. If it could produce sensations like that, and she could understand them, it was going to change things. What if the wave of feeling had been not relief, but hatred? Would she have ever got up again?

'Peaceful?' said the dinosaur.

'Peaceful,' said Jessica, and took from her bag the books she had brought with her.

The next couple of hours passed in as strange a piece of

education as the world has ever seen. Jessica knew how to communicate words – English and Drama, which Harriet Bray taught her at school were her best things. The dinosaur understood feelings and had twigged that the sounds the creature made were a substitute for these, and could mean things' names as well. So off they went.

Jessica started with the family photograph album. 'This,' she said, 'is me. It's awful of me, but you can *just* recognize it. I'm squinting a bit because of the sun, and it's my worst pair of trousers.'

The dinosaur wondered what the picture was. It was of something the same shape as the creature, but much smaller, and flat. Perhaps it was one of the creature's seeds? Perhaps the creature wanted to be rolled on and squashed and made to look like the picture. It was pointing at itself and at the picture, so it could mean that. But this seemed such a drastic course of action that the dinosaur decided to wait for clearer instructions before committing herself.

Jessica went through several pictures of herself, Fergus and Tim, and some of Billy and Dixie making faces. The dinosaur looked interested, and waited for the light of understanding to dawn. Finally she decided to try a little communication of her own, and aimed at Jessica one of the emotions she'd felt the day before. Again Jessica was bowled over, by a jumble of waves this time. She too thought back to yesterday as she picked herself up.

'Confusion?' she asked.

That was the word, the dinosaur remembered and repeated it.

In her bag Jessica had brought a pad of paper and a black felt-tip. She put away the photographs, and got out the drawing things. Looking intently at the dinosaur, she drew quite a good outline of it, thinking hard about it as she did. She let the dinosaur watch the picture grow, and when it was done she pointed to its feet and to the feet on

the drawing, at its head and to the head on the drawing.

In the dinosaur's brain, a gleam of light appeared.

'Brilliant?' it said.

'Exactly,' said Jessica, and quickly drew an outline of herself next to the dinosaur.

'Jessica,' she said, but the dinosaur did not repeat it. She had seen this drawing lines business before, and was remembering it. With her nose she drew a shape on the floor of the cavern – one circle surrounded by another. She had drawn it before and never forgotten it. 'That's a polo mint,' said Jessica.

'Polomint,' said the dinosaur, and stored away the information. So, the spaceship the silver creatures had visited in when she was small was called a polomint. It might come in useful, you never know.

Now the connection between picture and word was established, Jessica returned to the photo album – this time with great success. Each child was identified, named and its name repeated. The dinosaur learned, 'Dad, Mum, house, tree, car, school,' and managed to get them right when Jessica changed the order.

Then Jessica did a brave thing. She read the dinosaur *The Wind in the Willows* and *Hamlet*. Not all of them – just the bits in both that Harriet had underlined for her, with the words, 'This is good writing' in the margin. Some bits had, 'Copy out and learn' next to them. Harriet was a rather old-fashioned teacher, but had taught Jessica well, and Jessica had a marvellous time being, in turn, a water-rat and the Prince of Denmark with all the feeling she could muster.

The dinosaur applied her brain to Jessica's words. All we know about a dinosaur's brain is that it's smaller than ours – about the size of an egg. We also know that there are about nine tenths of our brains that we can't get at, so don't use. It's quite likely dinosaurs are the same, with a bit of brain for language and speech that they hadn't needed until now. I'm assuming that's the case anyhow.

Knowing nothing about language, the dinosaur didn't know Shakespeare was harder than Kenneth Grahame (he's the man who wrote *The Wind in the Willows*). So she listened to both with equal intensity, and stored them away in her almost empty memory.

After two hours, Jessica stopped.

'That's enough Shakespeare for now,' she said (for playing all the parts in *Hamlet* is quite tiring).

The dinosaur looked at her. 'The rest is silence?' she said.

Jessica was amazed. 'You *were* listening!'

'Ay, marry,' said the dinosaur. 'Poop, poop!'

'And do you understand everything now?' asked Jessica.

'When the wind's in the south,' said the dinosaur importantly, 'I can tell a hawk from a handsaw.'

'Excellent,' said Jessica, 'then look at this.'

'This' was Tim's project. Jessica took the dinosaur through it, and the dinosaur corrected a few points, meticulously. The only stumbling block was the word 'extinct' which Jessica had to explain over and over again. 'Not extinct,' said the dinosaur, and tried to turn some pages over. Jessica turned them for her, until they got to Tim's picture of the Loch Ness monster. 'There,' said the dinosaur. 'Not extinct.'

'It's only a legend,' said Jessica.

The dinosaur looked at the end of her leg. They hadn't done that word yet. 'More,' she said, 'Poop, poop!'

Next on Jessica's agenda was a map of the British Isles. She spread it out. 'Us,' she said, 'here is Clademouth. This is England. This is land. This is sea. Where the boats are.'

'There is nothing,' said the dinosaur, 'quite like messing about in boats.'

'Well done,' said Jessica.

'Um – . . . Loch Ness?' said the dinosaur, casually.

'Up here,' said Jessica, and the dinosaur stored away in her brain the spot Jessica had pointed to on the map next to Hamlet's soliloquy and Dixie's name, because she hadn't really got a filing system going yet. Jessica went on.

'I want you to see the map, and know all these things so you can look after yourself. You see, you may have to go away from here. The grown-ups might find you, and might not understand. I probably won't be able to warn you in time. You'll have to trust your instinct.'

'Extinct?' asked the dinosaur.

'Instinct. But if your instinct gets it wrong, extinct is what you'll be. But I think you'll know when. Oh, by the way – I'm leaving you this.' She put down the radio, switched to Radio Sun. 'We want you to understand modern English. It's not as good as Shakespeare, but more people speak it.' And with this, Jessica picked up the alarm clock, wound it up again and buried it just below the surface. She kissed the dinosaur on the nose and turned to go. Suddenly she thought she might not see it again.

'Jessica?' said the dinosaur. They each had a tear in their eyes. 'Sorrow. Brilliant sorrow.' Jessica walked out of the cavern, thinking of ways to explain her long absence to Mum.

SIX

A REPLACEMENT NEWSPERSON – FURTHER HURRICANES – A HERO
ARRIVES – ALARM BELLS SOUND.

The news on the radio was being read by Janice. Simon had overslept. Janice had crept out of the flat to the radio station and seized her opportunity. The morning bulletin was due. Simon was not there, Janice was. Janice had read the morning bulletin cheerfully and briskly, stumbling only over the new Russian president's name (which was Mrs Galitzneyetitcheff, so she had a good excuse) and saying 'nucular' twice instead of 'nuclear'. But by lunchtime Janice was Radio Sun's new newsreader and Simon (who had only just arrived at work) was reduced to introducing 'Sounds of the Eighties'. Funnily enough the staff of Radio Sun referred to 'Sounds of the Eighties' as 'Dinosaur's Hour' because it was aimed at older listeners. The staff (and Simon) would have been pretty surprised to know that on that particular day a dinosaur was actually listening to it.

The green light went on and Janice spoke.

'Five o'clock newstime on Radio Sun. Janice Reeves your newsperson bringing you all you need to know about all you need to know. First of all the hurricane clearing-up operation, which has been going according to plan. Chief Executive of Clademouth Council, Bill Todmore, said today that the response from the public had been what they had come to expect from Clademouth people, so extra forces were being brought in from outside.

'Latest reports say that Clademouth Third School should re-open tomorrow morning, when power is restored. Most homes now have power again. And Mrs Johnson's cat Jeffrey has been found. He'd been trapped under a fallen greenhouse, and was discovered when Mr Johnson was tidying up. The cat was evidently very frightened and distressed and Mr Johnson has been treated for minor cuts and abrasions but good news anyway that someone benefitted from the greenhouse effect.'

(Janice's producer gave her a thumbs up through the control room window. In the next studio Simon ground his teeth.)

'Now to Clademouth's bomb. The five hundred pound Second World War German bomb positively identified by Mr Neil Bridges of Channel View Close is to be defused tomorrow by a detachment from the Peace Corps. According to Mr Bridges it must have been dropped on Clademouth in about 1941 by the Luftwa . . . Luftwa . . . I'm sorry, I think it's Lufthansa but anyway it was the Germans.

'A look at the weather for the next few days. Well, the Peace Corps had better get to that bomb quickly while the cliff's still there because we have a low of 933 minibars out in the Atlantic and that could just mean more of the same. It's going to be really, really windy sometime in the next couple of days, so if you're out at sea better button down those hitches. That's all from the newsroom. I'm Janice Reeves. Here's Simon Hinch back with "Sounds of the Eighties". What have you got for us this evening, Simon?'

'A poisoned dagger,' thought Simon, but played a Cliff Richard eightieth birthday record instead.

The next morning a convoy of Electrovers arrived from the Peace Corps. They were camouflaged in light green, dark green and grey (though England had been yellow and brown for some time now). Still, as the soldiers said, it made them easier to see, which was a plus.

Major Floyd could quite possibly have been a nice man if, instead of becoming a Major, he had become, say, a miner. But a Major he was, so he put his foot in it first and didn't ask questions afterwards. Major Floyd was twenty-nine, which is young for a Major, but at various stages of his army life he had become confused and run towards the enemy when everyone else was running away, so they had had to give him several medals and promotion. His first name was Torquil, and he thought none of his men knew this. They all did. They thought Major Torquil Floyd was an idiot, from his Dumbo ears to the sandy tufts of hair on his cheekbones and his eyes like two blue marbles set in meringue.

'This is the place,' said Major Floyd, raising his leather stick to halt the convoy. 'I say,' he shouted to a passer-by, 'This is Clademouth Cliff, isn't it?'

The passer-by gave them meticulous directions so it wasn't *his* fault that Major Floyd and his men took four hours to cover the next twenty miles to Clademouth.

Neil Bridges met them outside the Duck of Windsor. He had got a message that they might be late from Major Floyd himself. It was a bit faint, for the Major had forgotten to extend the aerial of his personal communicator. But by twelve-thirty Mr Bridges was leading them down the cliff – Major Floyd, four soldiers and his Sergeant. (The Sergeant had four fingers missing on his right hand, which made people treat him with great respect. The sergeant never told anyone he had lost them during his first week in the army while peeling potatoes, so his reputation for bravery remained intact.)

The children, and quite a lot of the population, tried to follow. Major Floyd turned and addressed them.

'Ladies and Gentlemen,' he bellowed, 'I must ask that you keep well clear and don't attempt to come near to, down or around or up the cliff. We don't yet know the nature of the device in there but if it's anything like the average bomb it could be really quite . . . er . . . explosive. If for any reason it should explode it could cause death or even injury over a very widespread area, so for your own safety I must ask that you turn round and go back to a point at least 400 metres away.'

The crowd listened to this eminently sound advice, nodded to each other, waited until the Major's party had reached the bottom of the cliff and entered the cavern, then all moved forward again. They stood on the cliff edge, those at the front just able to see the 'Unexploded Bomb' sign. Tim and Fergus and Jessica and Dixie and Billy climbed down. The Sergeant shouted at them. 'Clear off!' he said. 'It's all right,' said Fergus, 'We found the bomb.' The Sergeant made what would have been a rude gesture if he'd had more fingers and followed Major Floyd into the cavern.

'This way,' said Mr Bridges, though there wasn't any other way they could have gone.

'I must ask you,' said Major Floyd, 'to leave once you have indicated the position of the device.'

'Don't you worry,' said Mr Bridges. 'You won't see me for dust.'

'Listen!' said one of the soldiers.

It was unmistakable – the rhythmic ticking of the alarm clock. They all heard it.

'Could have hours to go yet,' said Major Floyd.

'I doubt it,' said Mr Bridges. 'It was ticking two days ago. And in any case you chaps always arrive when it's just about to blow up and defuse it two seconds before it does. I've seen it in films.'

Major Floyd gave him a withering look which was wasted in the darkness, and they moved slowly forward.

At the other end of the cavern, Tim was climbing down the clay slope. He dared not use the torch, because the bomb squad would see it. But the cavern seemed much larger than yesterday, and more light and airy. He hid behind a rock as he heard the Major's and Mr Bridges' voices.

'Here we are,' said Mr Bridges. 'Just here.'

'Where?' said Major Floyd. 'Here, get that floodlight on, Sergeant.'

There was a clatter, a curse, another clatter and the cave was filled with light. And that was all it was filled with. A huge, empty cavern with four soldiers and a science teacher at one end. And a small boy, who could not help coming out from behind his rock, so great was his surprise.

'Where's the dinosaur?' said Tim. And at that point the alarm clock went off.

SEVEN

The biggest problem for the dinosaur was finding things to hide behind. At the moment she wasn't hiding behind anything. She was one extra sand dune among many, about two miles along the coast from the cavern. She had covered herself in sand just as the sun came up, and then sat very still. Some children were playing on her. They had waved to Major Floyd as he drove past, and again ten minutes later when he drove past in the opposite direction, having got more instructions from more passers-by. The children tickled – especially when they tried to dig holes in her back with their little spades.

She had waited for some hours after Jessica left before making her move. She now knew all of Radio Sun's jingles, and had heard (with varying degrees of interest) a gardening programme, a phone-in about organic washing powder, Holiday Round-up, Your Money and You (a bar of chocolate was now twelve Ecus-fifty, interest rates were at 19.5% and the Bankses, who were not rich, would have been worth over a million pounds if there had still been pounds). Then she had watched the air grow cold through the gap in the front of the cavern. When she could see almost no heat at all, she had pressed the button on the radio that Jessica had pressed (a dinosaur's tongue is forked, and very sensitive, so precise movements like this are no problem to it).

It is time, I think, that we knew a little more about our dinosaur. First, her eyesight. As well as light, which *we* see, a dinosaur sees heat, like a snake. A snake sees everything in terms of its temperature, and knows hot things

49

are dangerous. If ever you are near a snake and it looks like striking, shut your eyes and your mouth. These are much the hottest bits of you, and if you hide them the snake doesn't know where you are.

The dinosaur saw both heat and light. She had seen the children as shapes, but warm shapes. Their photographs in the album were the same shapes, but cold, so she found it hard to connect them. Jessica's drawings were warmer, and made things clear.

A dinosaur's ribs are very flexible. By being light and bendy, they can move between trees more easily than if they were heavy and stiff. So the entrance to the cavern, though only about two metres wide, was not an impossible barrier. By the time she was out it was, admittedly, a couple of metres wider, and a good deal of rubble had been dislodged, but the dinosaur was out in the open air. Her ribs were a little sore, she was hungry and confused, but she was free. And there has never been a living thing on earth that did not value freedom. She set off along the beach – the cold sea on her left, the warmer cliffs on her right, and occasional moonlight above as the clouds raced across the sky. It was still very windy – windy enough to discourage late-night walkers from coming out on to the cliff and wondering why a dinosaur was walking along the beach.

She did meet a dog, which barked furiously. The dinosaur decided that the noisy, hot thing spoke very bad English but was not dangerous. The dog got bored and went away, thinking that the Rottweiler breeders had really got it right this time. It sniffed the enormous dropping the dinosaur had left to show she was in charge of the beach, and lifted its leg against it. Three flies had the biggest party of their lives on the top.

You may think that the dinosaur was adapting amazingly well to her new surroundings, for one who had been asleep for 125 million years and had found things quite different when she woke up. Well, let me just say that I am pretty impressed as well. But it's actually quite likely that she would have done well: the most powerful instinct in any of us is self-preservation – the instinct not to become extinct. We know the dinosaur was a creature of instinct rather than intellect (so is a dog or a horse). And instinct told her that to stay alive she must remember all the information Jessica had given her, and store it in her brain. She hadn't had to use her brain much before, but it was there, ready for use in the future, and it *was* the future now, and she was using it. It was the size of a chicken's egg. She knew this from reading Tim's project, though she had not yet seen a chicken.

What it comes down to is that she wanted to stay alive, so she made a big effort to learn. Anyone can learn things when they want to.

So, after a great deal of thought, the dinosaur decided she should walk through the night and, as she felt the warmth of the approaching sun curve over the horizon, she made herself into a sand dune and went to sleep.

Mr Bridges thought Major Floyd was being unnecessarily rude. He wished he'd shut up, so that Mr Bridges could run after Tim and check that he had said what he thought he'd said. Tim had turned and run out of the cavern's other entrance as fast as he could – not just to escape the grown-ups, but to tell the other children.

Major Floyd waved the alarm clock under Mr Bridges' nose. 'Fifty-six miles,' he said. 'Fifty-six miles to defuse a bloody alarm clock.'

'It's only twelve miles to the barracks, sir,' said one of the soldiers.

'Fifty-six miles. You look on the milometer. Fifty-six miles of tension for me and my men. Thousands of Ecus' worth of sensitive equipment sitting out there. All for some twit who can't tell a bomb from an alarm clock.'

'There *was* a bomb,' said Mr Bridges. 'I saw it. It was grey, and shaped like a bomb.'

'I know what shape a bomb is, sunshine,' said Major Floyd in his nastiest voice. 'And I haven't seen that shape in here.' And he turned on his heels, and in quite a short time (after walking confidently into a few cracks in the cavern walls) found the exit in the cave. He led his men out, and climbed the cliff to tell the public that all was well, false alarm, no need for panic. The public walked away, disappointed and cold from standing on a cliff top on a windy day waiting for a huge bang and bits of Major Floyd to fly past. Instead all they got was all of Major Floyd walking past, climbing into his Electrover and leading his crack team of experts off in all directions.

In the cavern, Mr Bridges started searching. He had seen a bomb. It was grey. It was shaped like a bomb. Or, of course, like the tail of a dinosaur.

Mr Bridges had heard what Tim said. He had guessed the wrong end of the dinosaur, but he was dangerously close.

The dinosaur sat immobile in the evening sun. On her back was an abandoned sandcastle, with a small European flag fluttering wildly at the top. She wasn't restless. Her heartbeat was down to about ten a minute and she was, in effect, hibernating for a day. A lot of animals can do this. It saves their energy, and means they have to eat less. It also means that not much oxygen gets to the brain at these times. So rather than wondering what Hamlet would do in the circumstances, the dinosaur was back with good old instinct. Stay alive. Do not move. Movement dangerous. Hungry. Must eat. Do not move.

When it was very dark, at about one o'clock in the morning, she moved. Scattering sand, flags, abandoned buckets and spades, she rose to her feet and headed inland. It was still windy, and the wind came off the sea so brought no helpful foody smells with it. But the dinosaur could see ahead a hot place. It was a farmer's silage clamp, steaming with rotting hay waiting for Clademouth's cattle to come and eat it in the winter. The dinosaur found it delicious, once she had learnt to spit out the old car tyres that held its tarpaulins in place. She ate half a tonne, and walked away feeling full, well and dangerously confident.

Not everybody is asleep at one o'clock in the morning. The first person who wasn't asleep was a fourteen year-old boy on his way home from a party. He was carrying the last of a six-pack of extra-strong Rambo lager, the other five of which were inside him. Well, had been inside him, because he'd been sick in someone's garden on the way home. The way home included a short cut through the very farmyard where the dinosaur was wolfing down cattle fodder. The boy stopped, watched, stared at the can of lager, and watched the dinosaur again.

The hurrying clouds had exposed the moon at that moment, and the dinosaur showed very clearly – a large, extinct herbivore busily herbivoring a lot of herbs. The boy dropped the can and ran, swearing never to drink again until he was at least fifteen. The dinosaur saw him only as a scampering warm thing, and thought little of it.

The second person who wasn't asleep was the farmer's wife. A happy, apple-cheeked woman by day, she spent her nights in an agony of indecision, looking first at the ceiling, then at the sleeping farmer, then at the ceiling. The farmer was a happy, apple-cheeked man by day and night. His wife, for twenty years, had lain awake most of the night wondering why she wasn't happy with him. Some nights she got up and stared out of the window. Tonight she didn't, though the top of the dinosaur's back passed just below the first floor sill as she made her way back to the sand dunes. Seeing it wouldn't have made her happy.

The third, fourth and fifth people who weren't asleep

were washing. Cheap water came on at midnight and went off at 5 a.m., so many people rose then in order to have the luxury of a hot bath. Since the greenhouse effect had taken a proper grip, England's water supply was in a terrible state. Spain had always been hot, and took its water from underground where the sunshine could not steal it. England, new to this heat, still had a system of open Victorian reservoirs which the sun gradually evaporated, and which the winds stole to drop on distant, Far Eastern swamps. So water was rationed, and baths were economical only during the middle of the night when the cheap rate was on. The third, fourth and fifth people were, therefore, all in the bath when the dinosaur passed. One of them thought she heard something.

The sixth person was a milkman. The last of the dawn patrol, since the fax machine had done away with the postman, the milkman still delivered milk to Clademouth before it was fully light. He saw the dinosaur clearly, smelt its silage breath as it passed a metre from him. The dinosaur didn't see him. It was getting light quicker than she wished. She was full of food, her heart was up to speed and her brain was bubbling with oxygen. She must become a sand dune again. Quickly. The milkman did not follow her. He watched where she went. He was a sober, sensible man who could remember the milk orders for a whole street. He was just the sort of witness the dinosaur didn't need.

EIGHT

THE INTERROGATION OF TIM – DISCOVERY OF A LOST MERCEDES
– CONFESSION – THE CHILDREN DISAPPEAR.

'He can't have said "dinosaur",' said Dad.
     'He did say "dinosaur",' said Mr Bridges.

They were sitting in the bar of the Duck of Windsor, wondering why all their efforts to make life as boring as possible hadn't worked. If you got up in the morning and did exactly what you did yesterday it should make everything stay the same. Then on Saturdays and Sundays you got up later, had different breakfasts and did different things, and the world was allowed to change very slightly as long as it remembered that on Monday it had to go back to normal again. All Dad and Mr Bridges had done was to go on in their grooves, burning their share of energy, eating their share of hard-won food, throwing away the things they didn't need. And the world rewarded them with drought, pollution, hurricanes, Major Floyd, disappearing bombs and small boys who said, 'Where's the dinosaur?'

'Have you asked him about it?' said Mr Bridges.

'Of course not,' said Dad testily. 'You've only just told me he said it.' Dad had had a hard day at his work station, re-writing the 'After the Hurricane' piece that the computer had mysteriously wiped. He had rung Neil Bridges to ask him for colourful details of the defusing of the bomb, and found that his front page story had gone up in smoke. The *Clarion* had had to go to press with a picture of a budgerigar sitting on a rabbit's head, and a report about Terry Curry, an England batsman, scoring forty-three against the Falklands in the Test Match. Terry Curry's aunt lived in Moors Avenue in the Care Centre, which was sufficient connection for Dad to have put in Terry's achievement under the headline 'Clademouth Curry gets runs'. (The story contained an interview with Rosemary Curry (77). When asked about her nephew's achievements she said, 'That'll be Sarah's boy. I saw him when he was eight. He broke the potting-shed window with that football of his. I blame his father.')

For the next few days there would be no shortage of front-page news for the *Clarion*, but Dad didn't yet know that. At the moment it was 6.30p.m., and Neil Bridges had just told him that his son, on seeing the empty cavern, had said, 'Where's the dinosaur?' Which meant that:

(1) His son had gone mad.

(2) Neil Bridges had gone mad.

or (3) There had been a dinosaur in the cavern.

Secretly, and although he was his best friend, Dad thought (2) was the most likely. It was working with all those chemicals that did it. But knowing Tim to be a truthful boy, there was a terrible possibility that (3) was the answer, and Dad didn't really feel equipped to deal with it if it was.

Back at the house the children were crammed into Jessica's room. So crammed that some of the toy animals had to sit on top of the wardrobe.

'It just came out,' said Tim, 'I didn't mean to say it.'

'They'll all want to look for it now,' said Billy.

'Any of us could have blurted it out,' said Jessica.

'We'd have had more sense,' said Dixie.

'*I*,' said Tim, 'would have had more sense than to set the alarm clock before I buried it. You can make them not go off, you know.'

'Look,' said Fergus. 'It's done now, and Mr Bridges must have heard it, and must have told someone.'

'They won't believe him,' said Billy. 'He was the one who identified the bomb that wasn't there.'

'That's true,' said Jessica.

'No, it's not,' said Dixie. 'Grown-ups don't count mistakes like that, 'cause they all make them.'

'Look,' said Fergus. (He always did.) 'Tim said it, and we can't alter that. What we've got to do is find the dinosaur before they do, and warn it.'

Jessica looked warmly at her brother. He might not have much sensitivity or imagination but he could cut through to the middle of a problem.

'It shouldn't be very hard to find,' she said. 'I seem to remember it being quite big.'

'Tim!'

The voice came from the hall. The children froze.

'Could you come down here for a moment, please?'

Like a medieval knight about to enter the lists with only a dustbin lid and a broom handle as weaponry, Tim rose and left the room.

Dad was in the hall with Neil Bridges and Mum. They were smiling in that frightening way that people do when they want to seem kind. Tim's legs felt like slime.

'Tim, old chap,' said Dad, smiling furiously. 'Pop down and have a word.'

Tim popped down, and they had several.

The other children followed, and ranged themselves round the door of the sitting-room so they could hear what was going on.

'Now then, Tim,' said Dad, 'sit you down.'

Tim sat down on the sofa, which was squidgy enough to suck your bottom down into it and pull your legs off the floor so you were nearly lying on your back. He hid his hands, as people do when they're frightened, by shoving them down between the sofa cushions. Dad was opposite him, his head silhouetted against the light from the window, with Mum and Mr Bridges either side of him like three shadow puppets. Tim could not see their faces, which were still making encouraging smiling curves as though they'd sellotaped the sides of their mouths upwards.

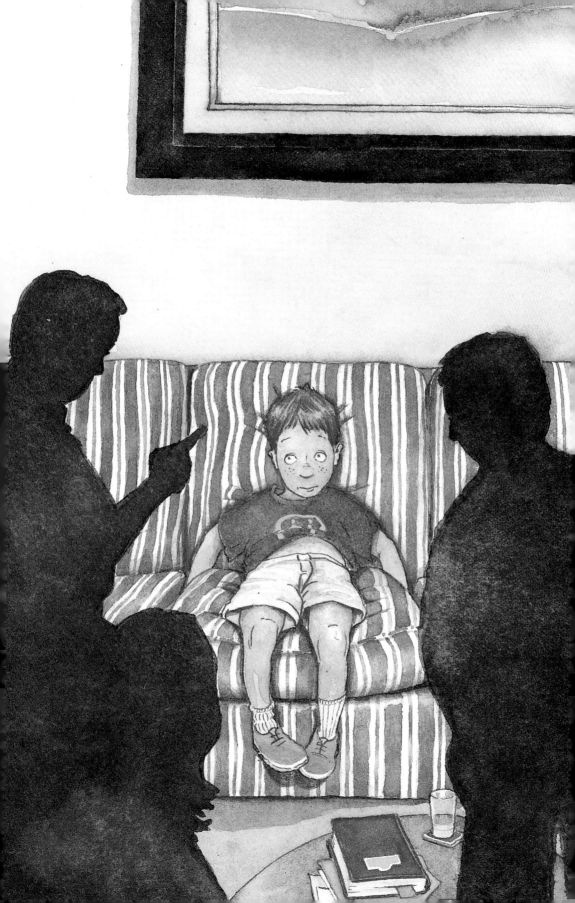

Mum spoke. 'Mr Bridges says that you were in the cavern when the Major was defusing the bomb. Were you in there, darling?'

'Yes,' said Tim, about as loudly as a shy lady shrew accepting a proposal of marriage.

'That could have been very dangerous,' said Mr Bridges. 'The bomb could have gone off with all of us in there.'

Mr Bridges still hoped really that somehow there *had* been a bomb, and it had just walked away. Tim – truthful Tim – dashed that hope as he began to seal the dinosaur's fate.

'It couldn't have been dangerous,' he said, 'because I knew there wasn't a bomb.'

'Did you say "dinosaur"?' asked Dad.

'No, bomb,' said Tim, who thought he'd spoken quite clearly for someone who had to use a throat that his heart kept trying to jump out of.

'I mean in the cavern. Earlier,' said Dad. 'When you saw it empty. Did you say, "Where's the dinosaur?"'

Tim didn't answer. His scrabbling fingers between the cushions had just discovered the toy Mercedes 750SE coupé that had been missing since Boxing Day. He had lost it after twenty-four hours of ownership and now its unmistakeable shape was firmly in his right hand. He couldn't help being more interested in this than in the black tribunal staring at him out of the sun.

'I've found my Mercedes,' he said.

'Impossible,' said Mr Bridges, 'I can't have got it that wrong. I couldn't have mistaken "I've found my Mercedes" for "Where's the dinosaur?"'

'Where is this Mercedes, Tim?' said Mum, gently and patiently, as though to rambling old Rosemary Curry in the Care Centre.

'Under this cushion,' said Tim.

The boy's gone mad, thought Dad. What a relief. Neil

Bridges was sane. There was no dinosaur. Now he must do everything he could to help his son.

'Will you show it to us, Tim?' he wheedled.

'Here,' said Tim, 'I lost it on Boxing Day.' He held up the small silver model.

'Tim,' said Mr Bridges, 'why did you say, "Where's the dinosaur?"'

'Because it had gone,' said Tim.

'Gone from where?' said Mum.

'From the cavern. Where we all found it.'

'When?'

'During the night, I s'pose.'

'No, when did you find it?' This was Dad, shattered again after thinking everything was all right.

'After the hurricane. The morning after. We climbed down the cliff . . .'

'You're not allowed on the cliff,' said Mum automatically.

'Sorry,' said Tim. 'We climbed down the cliff and found this cavern. We looked in it and it was dark so we switched on the torch . . .'

'The big kitchen torch?' said Mum incredulously.

'Sorry,' said Tim. 'We switched on the torch and went in and found this dinosaur. It was brilliant. We didn't want anyone to know so we made it disguise itself as a bomb and Mr Bridges thought it was a bomb but it must have known it wasn't safe because when he went in there with that soldier it had gone off.'

The boy's gone potty, thought Dad. I was right.

'What d'you mean, it had gone off?' asked Mum.

'The dinosaur,' said Tim. 'Gone off somewhere else.'

'Was it *alive*?' said Mr Bridges.

'Course it was,' said Tim. Grown-ups did say stupid things sometimes. 'It talked to us. It said "Peaceful". I wasn't frightened of it at all, except when it fell over.'

'Tim,' said Dad seriously. 'You have climbed on the cliff, which is against orders. You have gone into a dangerous

place, which you are not allowed to go into . . .'

'Taking the big kitchen torch,' added Mum.

'. . . taking the big kitchen torch. And you say you have met a live, talking prehistoric animal that has now disappeared.'

'Yes,' said Tim.

'How big was it?' said Mr Bridges.

'Why didn't you tell us?' said Mum.

'About thirty metres long,' said Tim, because Mr Bridges' question seemed the easier one to answer.

'Tim,' said Mum, 'why didn't you tell us?'

'We knew you'd be angry,' said Tim, and added, 'about us taking the big kitchen torch.' This wasn't why they'd kept the dinosaur a secret, but Tim couldn't tell them that the children hadn't dared trust the grown-ups to behave properly. It's not the sort of thing grown-ups like being told.

'Are you absolutely *sure*?' asked Mr Bridges.

'Yes,' said Tim. 'Last time we took it Mum was furious. Really, really angry.'

'Timothy Banks,' roared Dad. 'Did you or did you not see a live ruddy dinosaur?'

Tim cracked. The tears waterfalled down his cheeks, sobs shook his small body, and he howled, curling himself up and shutting his eyes to make himself invisible to grown-ups and snakes alike. Jessica and the other children burst into the room.

'Stop it!' she said. 'You're terrifying him.'

'Now look here, young lady . . .' said Dad, but got no further.

'Come on, Tim,' said Jessica. 'It's all right. Come with us.' And she took his hand and led her sobbing brother out of the room. The other children followed.

The grown-ups watched the door close behind them, and stood, dumbfounded. They didn't even move when Jessica came back into the room to retrieve the silver

Mercedes which Tim had left behind and to give her father a final withering look. Even when she had left for a second time, it was still six seconds before anyone spoke.

'Well!' said Dad.

'They're never like that,' said Mum. 'Never.'

'Thirty metres long,' said Mr Bridges.

'We still don't know,' said Dad. 'We don't actually know. About this dinosaur. We don't actually know if it's true.'

'Timothy never tells lies,' said Mum.

'Go and ask them,' said Mr Bridges.

'Only do it kindly this time,' said Mum. 'Without doing your smile.'

So Dad climbed the stairs, turned left, and knocked on Jessica's door.

In the sitting-room Mr Bridges looked at Mum, and wondered whether this would be a good time to put a comforting arm round her. With rare sensitivity he decided it wouldn't. Had he done so it would have confused things even further – especially because at that moment Dad came into the room.

'They've gone,' said Dad. 'The children. They're not there.'

NINE

DAD MAKES PEACE – PREPARATIONS FOR THE HUNT – MORE
DREADFUL WEATHER.

'Should we all go in opposite directions?' shouted Billy above the wind.

'No. Stick together,' said Fergus.

Tim squeezed Jessica's hand. He didn't want to go in opposite directions. They all set off along the beach.

'Look,' said Fergus, 'for dinosaur tracks. Footprints.'

They didn't find footprints, because the wind and tide had swept the beach four times since the dinosaur had walked along it. But they did find the dropping. Dixie saw it first.

'Yuck,' she said. 'Billy, come and look at this.'

'It's poo,' said Billy.

The lump smelt awful, unless you were one of the thousand flies walking about on it. As far as the flies were concerned the lump smelt of herbaceous borders, mint and bonfire smoke all rolled into one.

'Is it dinosaur poo?' asked Dixie, looking at Tim.

'I should think so,' said Tim, 'but I don't know. We aren't allowed to put poo in our projects.'

'Come on,' said Jessica. 'It must have been this way.'

'It's certainly been,' said Billy, holding his nose. They marched on.

They were among the sand dunes when Dad caught up with them.

'Jessica!' Dad shouted. 'Fergus! Tim!'

The children ignored him for as long as they thought they could get away with it, then stopped. Dad puffed up to them. 'Can we have a talk?' he asked. 'Please?'

'It's too windy to talk here,' said Jessica.

'All right. Come round here where it's sheltered,' said Dad, and led them round behind the largest of the sand dunes. 'Sit down, please,' he said, though being polite to the children was something he had not practised as much as he should. So they all sat down in the lee of a large sand dune and talked. (And I might as well say at this point that what you have just guessed about the sand dune is absolutely right, but don't rush ahead.)

'Dad,' said Jessica, 'I was rude to you back at the house, and I'm sorry.'

'But you *were* horrid to Tim,' said Fergus, inspired by Jessica's bravery.

'He was worried about things,' said Tim. 'He always shouts when he's worried.'

Billy and Dixie didn't say anything, because it wasn't *their* father sitting, small and crushed, on the sand. Instead they imagined that it was, and wondered if they'd be able to say those things to him.

'Can you just tell me what happened?' said Dad. Tim and Fergus looked at Jessica, who nodded and spoke.

'The morning after the hurricane we went to look at the cliff and found a cave. In the cave was a dinosaur – a live one. A Diplodocus. We spoke to it, and I gave it some lessons so it would understand what was going on. Now it's gone. That's all.'

'Why didn't you tell us?' said Dad.

'Because you'd have wanted to prod it or examine it or hurt it and put it in your silly paper.'

'It is *not* a silly paper,' said Dad.

'Look,' said Fergus. 'It has silly stories about donkeys and baby shows in it and nothing at all about big important things. It *is* a silly paper, Dad.'

'It's not even printed on recycled paper,' said Tim, much to his own surprise. But he felt much better after he said it, so it must have been all right.

'I don't know how you can do it,' said Jessica, warming

66

to her subject. 'Cut down millions of trees so that Clademouth *Clarion* readers can see pictures of themselves shaking hands with the Mayor or forgetting their words in *The Sound of Music*. It's typical. You pretend all the real problems aren't there, just like all grown-ups do. That's why we're in the state we are today, with hurricanes and no water and filth everywhere. Because grown-ups stuck their heads in the sand and hoped somehow things would sort themselves out.'

Anger had given Jessica's tongue wings and teeth, and the other children rewarded her with a small round of applause. The sand dune's instincts told it that on this occasion keeping its head in the sand was the right thing to do, and it kept very still.

Dad looked confused. It isn't easy to be told that what you had worked away at for twenty years was pointless. Particularly when you had always suspected that you were the only one who thought it might be pointless, while everyone else was impressed. Like a lot of people when they're confused, he did the wrong thing.

'How dare you?' he said. 'How dare you speak to me like that? You will all go home this instant, and I shall tell the authorities of your dinosaur, if it's true, and . . .'

'Of course it's true,' said Fergus. 'Just like everything Jessica was saying. Making your silly paper is destroying the world. Dinosaurs lived for 160 million years because they didn't have power stations and detergents and stupid local papers . . .'

'. . . with pictures of baby dinosaurs and advertisements for second-hand push-chairs,' said Billy. He then remembered that Dad wasn't his dad, but it was too late.

'Home!' roared Dad. 'Home. Now. All of you. Run!' He had not been so furious since an electric storm had erased the list of addresses on his computer. None of the people on the list had since got in touch with him, so he hadn't needed the list. But anger has nothing to do with logic.

The children got quickly to their feet, and set off briskly for home. They knew they'd said more than Dad's position allowed them to say, and they weren't surprised he was angry. They were surprised by just *how* angry, though, and a little frightened. The wind blowing flurries of sand into their faces didn't help, as they jogged back along the beach, Dad seething behind them.

The sand dune decided that if ever she met Dad she'd watch her step.

The phone was ringing when they got home. It was the *Clarion* office. The milkman had rung up to say he'd seen a Tyrannosaurus Rex. The father of the drunk fourteen-year-old had rung up to say his son had seen a sea-monster. Would Dad come in at once?

Dad put the phone down. So Tim hadn't been lying. He could see the headline. 'Clademouth family finds Dinosaur.' He'd show the children whether the *Clarion* had important stories in or not. Grabbing a coat, he went out into the gusty day, all thoughts of anger and the pain he'd caused the children put firmly behind him.

At Clademouth police station, decisions were being taken, and guns checked. The policemen looked forward to a dinosaur hunt. Probably a hoax, of course, but it would pass the time. And for a crack team of men and women used to sifting through dustbin loads of debris in search of a fragment of human tissue, finding forty tonnes of dinosaur should be easy. WPC Jenkinson suggested they took a magnifying glass, and PC Threlfall laughed a bit more than the joke deserved, because WPC Jenkinson had nice legs, even in her clumpy black shoes. PC Threlfall wouldn't have laughed so much if he'd known that twice the day before, while on beach litter patrol, he had walked heavily across the dinosaur's back.

The police waited for information. Dad rang the milkman. The farmer's wife rang nobody, for she had seen nothing. She was in the dairy connecting Friesian udders to Japanese milking machines. The Friesians were restless. She was sleepless. The dinosaur was still, unaware that the hunt might begin at any moment.

In any case the idea of a hunt did not frighten her greatly. The children had not prepared her for the ways of adults. Children, on finding a worm, will pick it up, examine it, or squat down and watch it. Then, as a rule, they let it go on its way. Adults will recoil in horror, or kill it. Or tread on it without noticing. Adults are frightened of things. Children are only interested in them, because they have not yet been told what to be frightened of.

Whatever happened when the grown-ups found the dinosaur and were frightened by it will have to wait, because at that moment, with a force more terrible than anything in any creature's memory, Clademouth was struck by the second hurricane. Far worse than the first, and in broad daylight.

TEN

IMPRESSIONS OF MODERN LIFE – REASONS FOR EXTINCTION
– COLD, UNHAPPY AND LOST.

The dinosaur felt the waves lash her back. They were mixed with pebbles – quite large pebbles – and sand and weed in a fierce, abrasive broth. She thought that among the sand dunes she was far enough inland to be safe from the sea. But here it was, whipping her back and screaming at her. She stayed still because it was daylight, and not safe.

Letting her thoughts wander round the newly-opened wing of her memory, she took stock of her situation. She thought of waking up in the cave, of meeting the children, of Jessica's lessons, of sand and silage clamps. And she tried to remember the time before she went to sleep for so many million years.

It hadn't been as exciting, she was sure of that. The dim images she was getting were of regularity, of days of plodding, herbivorous boredom. For she was walking the swamps long before the great carnivores. Tim's project had a picture from a Hollywood epic in which a Tyrannosaurus Rex had its jaws firmly sunk into a Diplodocus' neck. The dinosaur had been frightened by this – she had never seen, and could never have seen, a Tyrannosaurus Rex, for it would be another seventy million years after the time of the Diplodocus, before the fearsome beast evolved. She hoped she didn't meet one in Clademouth.

You must remember that until a couple of days ago the Diplodocus had never seen anything except swamps, trees, and other dinosaurs – Stegosaurus, Brachiosaurus, Iguanadon, though she had only just learned their names.

72

They had all tramped about eating trees, digesting trees and excreting trees and sleeping. That was it really. She had never seen the birds she was going to evolve into. She had never seen a woolly mammoth, a sabre-tooth tiger, a giraffe. Man's struggle to get to his feet, to make tools and develop speech – all these were new to her in the last two days. Flying machines above her head (though not going as fast as the silver creatures in their polo mint), electric cars, diesel lorries – all these had had to be squeezed into her little brain in a very short time.

Some things she couldn't understand at all. Why did some families have an extra four-legged child that was allowed to behave worse than the others? Why did men sit on the beach talking urgently into small black things held up to their ears? What were the couple on the next sand dune doing last night? The dinosaur had formed the impression it was something to do with breeding, in which case these creatures had certainly found a better method. A Diplodocus' sex life is too complicated to go into here, but revolves mainly round ways of getting twenty metres of tail out of the way, and usually makes both Diplodocuses so giggly that they have to stop. This may be why dinosaurs died out, though it's not the generally held theory.

Two things had impressed the dinosaur most. The children, and *Hamlet*. The children because they had been kind to something so big, and *Hamlet* because it made such a nice noise. Jessica had really meant whatever it meant, and the ferventness of her reading had gone straight to the dinosaur's heart. (Her brain may have been small, but her heart was the size of a small cow, and had beaten regularly once an hour throughout her long hibernation, keeping just enough blood trickling round her comatose body to stop it decaying.)

One thing had not impressed the dinosaur. That one thing was everything else except the children and Jessica's

reading. Given all the things that had happened to the planet since the dinosaur's swampy childhood, it didn't seem to be any more comfortable. It was noisy and smelly and there was an air of unease. A lot of things seemed to be lying about, discarded, that were made of valuable materials. There seemed little time for quiet contemplation, for thoroughly and deeply relishing the progress that had been made. The dinosaur had not, of course, been exposed to great music and art, which Jessica or Harriet would have said had the ability to bring order to the chaos. Had she been told this, the dinosaur's uncluttered brain would have said, 'Why did you make chaos in the first place?' and it's doubtful whether even Jessica or Harriet could have answered this.

The worst thing, she thought, was the climate. She didn't know that the human race itself was responsible. She couldn't. Jessica had not had time to show her all the pamphlets saying 'Save the tree', or explain the countless trees that had been pulped in order to print the pamphlets. Jessica had not had time to talk of carbon dioxide, effluent, poison, plutonium and global warming. And Jessica had not had time to explain about the differences between children and grown-ups, so the dinosaur did not know that, on meeting a dinosaur, grown-ups might behave in a stupider, more panic-stricken way than children.

She made a wrong decision. She decided that, daylight or no, she would get away from the huge waves and the bothersome wind and move inland.

It might, on reflection, have been better for the dinosaur if she had been frightened by grown-ups first and comforted by children later. As it was, she got the experiences the other way round, which made the frightening all the more frightening when it happened.

A hurricane whistling round her ears, she rose to her feet, a live Diplodocus 125 million years old. She did not know why she was alive, or why she was alone. Nobody does – though the best theories seem to be either a meteorite hitting the earth and destroying everything, or a rather complicated one about temperature and eggs. We know that if you change the temperature a snake lives in by only one degree it lays female eggs, instead of male and female eggs. Now whatever you think of fathers, they do have a role in keeping the species going. If there weren't any, a couple of generations and it would all be over. That may have been the dinosaur's fate. The planet warmed up, and it was suddenly all mum and no dad, so no babies. The planet was warming up now, too, which was why the hurricane was happening.

The dinosaur knew none of this. She was wet, cold and insecure as she walked past the wrecked barns of the farm, where this time the unhappy farmer's wife *did* see her. But she told no one.

It struck the dinosaur that she had no idea where the children lived.

ELEVEN

An hour after the hurricane struck, the children had no idea where they lived either. The wind tore the roof from their house and tossed it into the Clademouth shopping mall, where it destroyed a car parked in the pedestrian zone. The Banks family, re-united by crisis, had grabbed a few things and fought their way through air thick with bits of house, reaching Harriet's small bungalow fifty metres inland from their own. As Harriet forced the door shut behind them (for the hurricane seemed to want to come in as well) the cliff, with the Banks' house on it, collapsed into the sea, leaving no trace of the dinosaur's cavern or Neil Bridges' 'Unexploded Bomb' notice.

The next excitement of the day was meeting Simon Hinch, who they had heard on Radio Sun and seen once opening a Personal Transport Boot Sale, but never actually met. Harriet introduced them nervously, for she was aware that Simon's presence in the house (wearing only a towel) might lead them to jump to the right conclusion. The Duck of Windsor was pretty busy at the moment, for there was plenty to talk about. Harriet and Neil Bridges had gone in that lunchtime, and Mr Bridges had been so boring about his encounter with Major Floyd that Harriet had sent him home. Simon, seeing her now alone, had bought her a drink and poured out his woes about Janice, who was well on her way to being given the coveted breakfast show (a misnomer, since most people listened to it instead of, not with, breakfast). Each of them had lost someone, which gave them something in common and drew them close together, which is why, when the Banks family arrived in the early evening at Harriet's house, they met the formerly famous Simon Hinch holding a towel round his middle. He let go of it to shake hands, which in retrospect was a mistake.

The Clademouth Meteorological Society (which had seven members, six of whom had forgotten they *were* members, and was kept going only by the efforts of eighty-three-year-old Charles Templeton, with his rain-gauge, thermometer, anemometer, and various other ome-ters spread about his front room) had clocked up 92 miles per hour for the first hurricane. This second one managed to reach its century; 101 miles an hour of 85°-hot wind, spinning and twisting and heaving at all things made and grown as if weeding an enormous garden. Seaside trees are usually especially strong, for the wind tests their strength regularly and only the tough survive. After the two hurricanes, every tree in Clademouth higher than five metres lay on its side, bruised and confused.

To keep them company, the remaining electric power lines collapsed as well. That night there would be no street-lighting, no TV (though the underground cables with their twenty-eight channels still sent their game shows and Sumo wrestlers into people's homes, to meet cold TV sets gasping for power) no battery chargers for cars, no kidney machines in the health centre, no words in the memory of Robin Q. Banks' computer.

Had anyone wanted to heat their houses, they couldn't, because the gas main had blown up. This was, in fact, nothing to do with the hurricane. The gas main had lain unmaintained for as long as it could remember. No one likes being taken for granted, so on the day of the hurri-cane it took a deep breath and burst itself. Sadly, people were too busy to do much more than switch off the gas and surround the crater with traffic cones, which quickly blew away. The gas main sulked.

The school, which Radio Sun had so confidently predicted would soon re-open, was blown away completely. Fragmented and gone. Whole crescents of houses lost roofs, architectural details, chimneys and conservatories. Clademouth was the sort of place where home improvement was a way of life. In their leisure hours the men of Clademouth went hunting in the do-it-yourself hypermarkets outside the town, returning with fibreglass pillars and porches which they rawlplugged to the outside of their houses. Fake beams were added, dormer windows constructed in the roof to turn the loft into a room for Granny (whose arthritis meant getting up to her new eyrie was agonizingly painful). And almost everyone in Clade-mouth had a conservatory.

I think perhaps I haven't told you enough about the England that Clademouth was a part of. For a start, it was a little smaller than the England we know. People had moved out of Lincolnshire and parts of Norfolk, as the sea had begun to rise, swollen by the melted ice from the polar regions. The people of the earth had created for the planet a duvet of pollution that kept it warmer than it should have been. The ice began to melt, and the air became ever fouler. The sea's extra warmth was just what the chemicals and the sewage dumped in it wanted in order to fester more efficiently. They acted as fertilizers for the blue-green algae that bred as fast as mice.

The population had become resigned to all this. It was too late to do anything about it. Nobody put a figure on it, but privately people estimated mankind's lease on the planet to have hundreds of years to run rather than thousands. So some things ceased to matter. Like what to do about plutonium. Coal and oil had got the planet to a terminal state, nuclear power looked less dangerous than before, and dealing with thrown-away atomic waste was going to be a problem only after the planet was dead. So the nuclear programme was stepped up, and all went well until the Dungeness disaster. Dungeness is in Kent. Well, it was in Kent. It took quite a lot of Kent with it when it blew up. The rest of Kent, from Ramsgate across to Rye in Sussex, was now empty of life. There had been appalling riots as those on the edge of the affected area moved outwards, foraging for food and bringing radiation sickness with them. A cloud of radiation had been the last thing to travel through the Channel Tunnel, belching gamma rays across thousands of hectares of French farmland. Canterbury was empty, Dover destroyed. The new Archbishop of Winchester called for calm. The Government called for calm. Then the army ensured there was calm in the only way that armies understand. No one talked about it much now, because people don't want to remember days when brother kills sister, sister kills brother. They just squeezed up a little tighter on the remains of the hot, dry, sooty little island, and trusted each other slightly less.

None of which helped to keep people calm when hurricanes struck.

One effect of radiation and chemicals in the air and water was the rise to affluence of the conservatory salesmen. So almost everyone in Clademouth had a conservatory. It had double doors to act as an airlock, an ioniser, a soil purifier, and a blue light for zapping insects, and in it you could grow nice, predictable plants. Outside in the real air and the real soil plants grew to either a third or three times their normal size with no apparent rules. Wheat production in the South of England was vast, where the sun beat down and the electrons bounced through the eye-level ears of corn. Apples, on the other hand, were a thing of the past, for the water could no longer climb high enough from its subterranean home to lick the roots of the orchard.

On the day of the hurricane, each one of Clademouth's new conservatories took to the air, to join the plastic porches and dormer windows in a giant flying stampede

through the deserted streets. Not entirely deserted, for walking down the middle of the street was the dinosaur, covered in trees, broken glass and tomato plants.

She was seen by many people from their windows. Had telephone lines not been down, they would have rung each other to tell them. Had their homes not been falling about their ears they would have done something about it. One of them took a half-hearted shot at the dinosaur, and missed – which was quite skilful, given the dinosaur's size. But mainly they bothered with their own comprehensible problems, and left the incomprehensible monster to wander through the turbulent streets of Clademouth in search of the vibrations of Jessica, Fergus, Tim, Dixie and Billy.

The wind died as swiftly as it had grown. By the time people and the police dinosaur squad returned to the streets, the dinosaur had decided to start again from square one. She found the cliff where the cavern had been, and where the Banks's house had fallen along with its neighbours. She splashed through the huge breakers at the bottom of the new cliff face, trampling the Banks's furniture, but all the time sensing and smelling that these were things the children had known and used. This was where she had slept. It had moved about, but she knew this was the place. She looked up at the top of the cliff.

The Banks children had the same instinct. When the wind dropped, they set off to see how much damage had been done to their home, and to see if the dinosaur had returned. They found the new cliff top behind where their house had been, and looked over the edge to see both the debris and the Diplodocus. With a joyful whoop they climbed down the too-new-to-be-forbidden cliff towards her.

Mr Banks was not far behind. Harriet's house was too small not to notice when three noisy children left it. He heard the door shut in his subconscious. He noted the drop in sound level. He hardly noticed Harriet saying to Mrs Banks, 'Poor Simon, he fell over in the hurricane, he was covered in mud, he asked if he could have a shower.'

Suddenly Mr Banks shouted, 'They've gone!' And picking up the gun he had brought from home – for even when the enemy is a storm, men feel safer with a gun – he ran after them.

The children reached the bottom of the new cliff. The dinosaur cheerfully lumbered towards them. As Mr Banks reached the cliff top, that is what he saw. He did not sense friendship and trust. He thought a big beast was attacking his little cubs. The dinosaur saw him and raised an inquisitive head, and at that moment Mr Banks fired.

She felt the bullet pass into her head just to the right of her right eye. She did not know what a bullet was, but it hurt, and it burned, and it burned more, and it had come from the cold man at the top of the cliff holding the small, hot object.

With her burning eyes she stared at him. She remembered the face in Jessica's cold photograph, and recognized him.

'Dad,' she said.

Then she lost consciousness and fell.

TWELVE

THE DINOSAUR'S DISILLUSION – JESSICA'S FORGIVENESS – TIM'S
FURY – A SURPRISING END.

Jessica looked at the dinosaur lying still at her feet, then up at her father on the cliff top. He was shaking his head, as if to clear his ears of water after swimming. He stared at the gun, and for a terrible moment Jessica thought he was going to shoot himself. At that moment Dixie arrived beside him, gently took the gun and handed it to Mum, who had followed on behind with the others.

They stood silhouetted along the new escarpment – Mum, Harriet, Simon, Dixie, Dad, Billy, even Mr Bridges who had heard the shot and come running. Then Dad scrambled down the cliff to join his children.

'I thought it was going to hurt you,' he said to Jessica.

'I know. I understand.'

Jessica turned to the dinosaur's motionless head, and she and Fergus and Tim stroked it with their small hands.

'Oh, Brilliant,' said Fergus. 'Poor Brilliant.'

'It shouldn't have met us first,' said Tim. 'We were nice to it, so it thought it could trust people. If it had met a grown-up first it would have learned to be frightened.' And he looked up at his father with an expression of great, deep loathing, for he was not as wise as Jessica, and would take longer to find forgiveness.

Jessica looked at her brothers, and at the heaviest friend she'd ever had, and thought of the afternoon when she read *Hamlet* to it.

'Now cracks a noble heart,' she whispered. 'Good night, sweet prince, and flights of angels sing thee to thy rest.'

A Diplodocus's brain, as we know and have said often, is the size of an egg. Whatever limitations this gives the Diplodocus (and they can't have been very severe, for we also know that dinosaurs survived for 160 million years) it makes them quite hard to kill. Mr Banks missed the dinosaur's large heart, which had kept her ticking over beneath the cliff for 65 million years. The dinosaur, in other words, was not dead. She had a headache, and she had been briefly stunned, but she was alive.

She heard the gasp from the others as she raised her head. She sensed the love and relief that came from the children. She sensed the fear that came from the grown-ups. Identifying Dad, who was now standing nervously beside Jessica, she directed at him a feeling of hurt and anger that lifted him off his feet and drove him bodily five metres backwards. He struck his head on a rock as he

landed, and it was some days before he was well enough to start rebuilding relations with his family.

The dinosaur turned unsteadily towards the sea, and paused. Her long neck coiled towards Jessica, and she kissed her with her forked tongue.

'The rest,' said Brilliant the Dinosaur, 'is silence.'

It had never occurred to the children that she could swim. But swim she did, strongly and smoothly through the breakers and out to sea. Only when she could no longer feel their mixed emotions beaming out towards her did she change direction.

She remembered the map Jessica had shown her. She had listened hard. She submerged, turned right and swam off in what she hoped was the direction of Loch Ness.